For Suzanne

First published in hardback in Great Britain by HarperCollins Children's Books in 2007

3 5 7 9 10 8 6 4 2

ISBN 13: 978-0-00-718228-2
ISBN 10: 0-00-718228-7

Text and illustrations copyright © Oliver Jeffers 2007

Visit our website at: www.harpercollins.co.uk

Printed in Hong Kong by Printing Express Ltd.

The Way Back Home

Oliver Jeffers

HarperCollins *Children's Books*

Once there was a boy,

and one day, as he was putting
his things back in the cupboard,
he found an aeroplane.

He didn't remember leaving it in there but
he thought he'd take it out for a go right away.

The plane lifted off the ground
and up into the sky...

higher   and higher   and higher.

Suddenly the plane spluttered...

it had run out of petrol.

Now the boy was stuck on the moon.
What was he to do?

He was all alone and afraid
and soon his torch began to go out.

Up in space someone
else was in trouble too.

His engine had
broken down...

and steering the ship
towards a flicker of light,
he landed on the moon
with a bump.

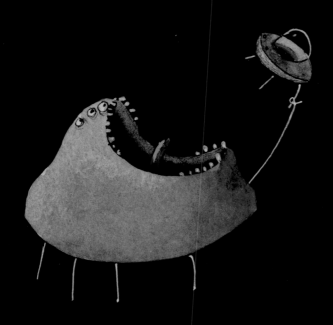

Both the boy and the Martian could
hear noises in the dark and both
feared the worst.

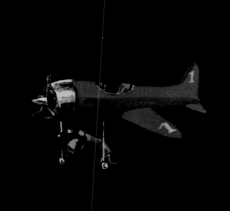

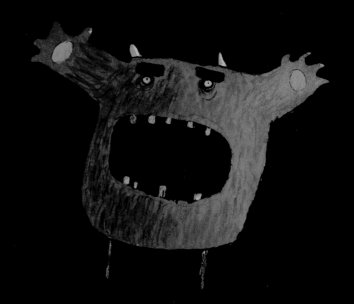

But as their eyes
got used to the dark,
they both realised
they'd met someone
else in trouble.

They weren't
alone any more.

The boy showed the Martian his empty petrol tank and the Martian showed the boy his broken engine.

Together they thought of ways to fix their machines and how to get them both back home.

The boy jumped down to
earth to get the things
they would need...

right

down

into

the

sea...

and swam towards home.

But by the time he got there, the boy was tired out so he sat in his favourite chair, just to catch his breath.

His favourite programme was just starting and he settled down to watch.

Suddenly he remembered what he should be doing and rushed off to the cupboard to get what he needed. He ran outside and shouted. But there was no reply, he couldn't be heard.

The boy
climbed to
higher ground,
called again,
and waited.

This time,
a rope
was lowered.

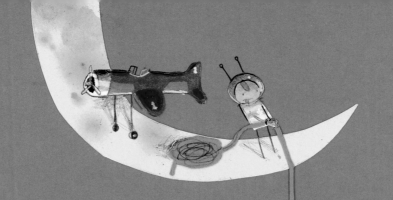

The boy
began to climb
and the Martian
began to pull,
and soon the
boy was back
on the moon.

The boy fixed up the Martian's engine
with the right spanner and the
Martian filled the boy's petrol tank.

They said goodbye and thanked
each other for their help.

They wondered if they'd
ever meet again.

After a long night
they were both finally
off the moon.

The boy went one way
and the Martian went
another, both on their
way back home.

*hello?
hello?*